THE WONDERFUL WIZARD OF OZ

VOL. 6

ADAPTED FROM THE NOVEL BY L. FRANK BAUM

Writer: ERIC SHANOWER
Artist: SKOTTIE YOUNG
Colorist: JEAN-FRANCOIS BEAULIEU
Letterer: JEFF ECKLEBERRY

Assistant Editors: LAUREN SANKOVITCH & LAUREN HENRY
Associate Editor: NATE COSBY
Senior Editor: RALPH MACCHIO

Special Thanks to Chris Allo, Rich Ginter, Jeff Suter & Jim Nausedas
Collection Editor: MARK D. BEAZLEY
Assistant Editors: NELSON RIBEIRO & ALEX STARBUCK
Editor, Special Projects: JENNIFER GRÜNWALD
Senior Editor, Special Projects: JEFF YOUNGQUIST
SVP of Print & Digital Publishing Sales: DAVID GABRIEL
Production: JERRY KALINOWSKI
Book Design: SPRING HOTELING

Editor in Chief: AXEL ALONSO
Chief Creative Officer: JOE QUESADA
Publisher: DAN BUCKLEY
Executive Producer: ALAN FINE

MARVEL

visit us at www.abdopublishing.com

Reinforced library bound edition published in 2014 by Spotlight, a division of the ABDO Group, PO Box 398166, Minneapolis, Minnesota 55439. Spotlight produces high-quality reinforced library bound editions for schools and libraries. Published by agreement with Marvel Characters, Inc.

Printed in the United States of America, North Mankato, Minnesota.
102013
012014
♻ This book contains at least 10% recycled materials.

3 1357 00067 9248

Library of Congress Cataloging-in-Publication Data

Shanower, Eric.
  The wonderful Wizard of Oz / adapted from the novel by L. Frank Baum ; writer: Eric Shanower ; artist: Skottie Young. -- Reinforced library bound edition.
     pages cm
  "Marvel."
  Summary: An eight-volume, graphic novel adaptation of L. Frank Baum's tales of Dorothy, a little girl from Kansas who is blown by a storm to the magical land of Oz, where she has amazing adventures while trying to get home.
  ISBN 978-1-61479-226-0 (vol. 1) -- ISBN 978-1-61479-227-7 (vol. 2) -- ISBN 978-1-61479-228-4 (vol. 3) -- ISBN 978-1-61479-229-1 (vol. 4) -- ISBN 978-1-61479-230-7 (vol. 5) -- ISBN 978-1-61479-231-4 (vol. 6) -- ISBN 978-1-61479-232-1 (vol. 7) -- ISBN 978-1-61479-233-8 (vol. 8)
  1. Graphic novels. [1. Graphic novels. 2. Fantasy.] I. Young, Skottie, illustrator. II. Baum, L. Frank (Lyman Frank), 1856-1919. III. Title.
  PZ7.7.S453Won 2014
  741.5'973--dc23
                    2013029128

All Spotlight books are reinforced library binding and manufactured in the United States of America.

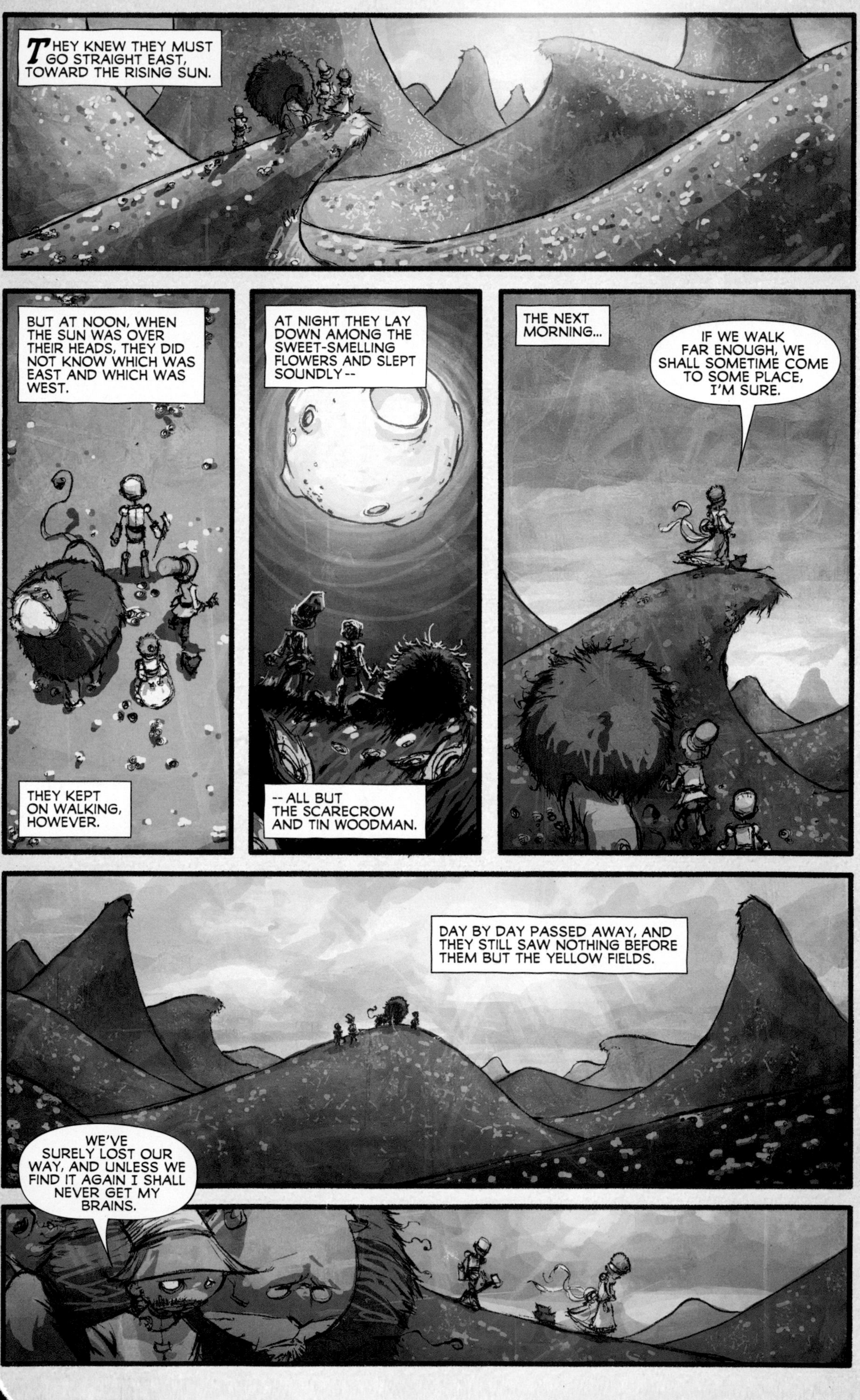
THEY KNEW THEY MUST GO STRAIGHT EAST, TOWARD THE RISING SUN.
BUT AT NOON, WHEN THE SUN WAS OVER THEIR HEADS, THEY DID NOT KNOW WHICH WAS EAST AND WHICH WAS WEST.
THEY KEPT ON WALKING, HOWEVER.
AT NIGHT THEY LAY DOWN AMONG THE SWEET-SMELLING FLOWERS AND SLEPT SOUNDLY--
-- ALL BUT THE SCARECROW AND TIN WOODMAN.
THE NEXT MORNING...
IF WE WALK FAR ENOUGH, WE SHALL SOMETIME COME TO SOME PLACE, I'M SURE.
DAY BY DAY PASSED AWAY, AND THEY STILL SAW NOTHING BEFORE THEM BUT THE YELLOW FIELDS.
WE'VE SURELY LOST OUR WAY, AND UNLESS WE FIND IT AGAIN I SHALL NEVER GET MY BRAINS.

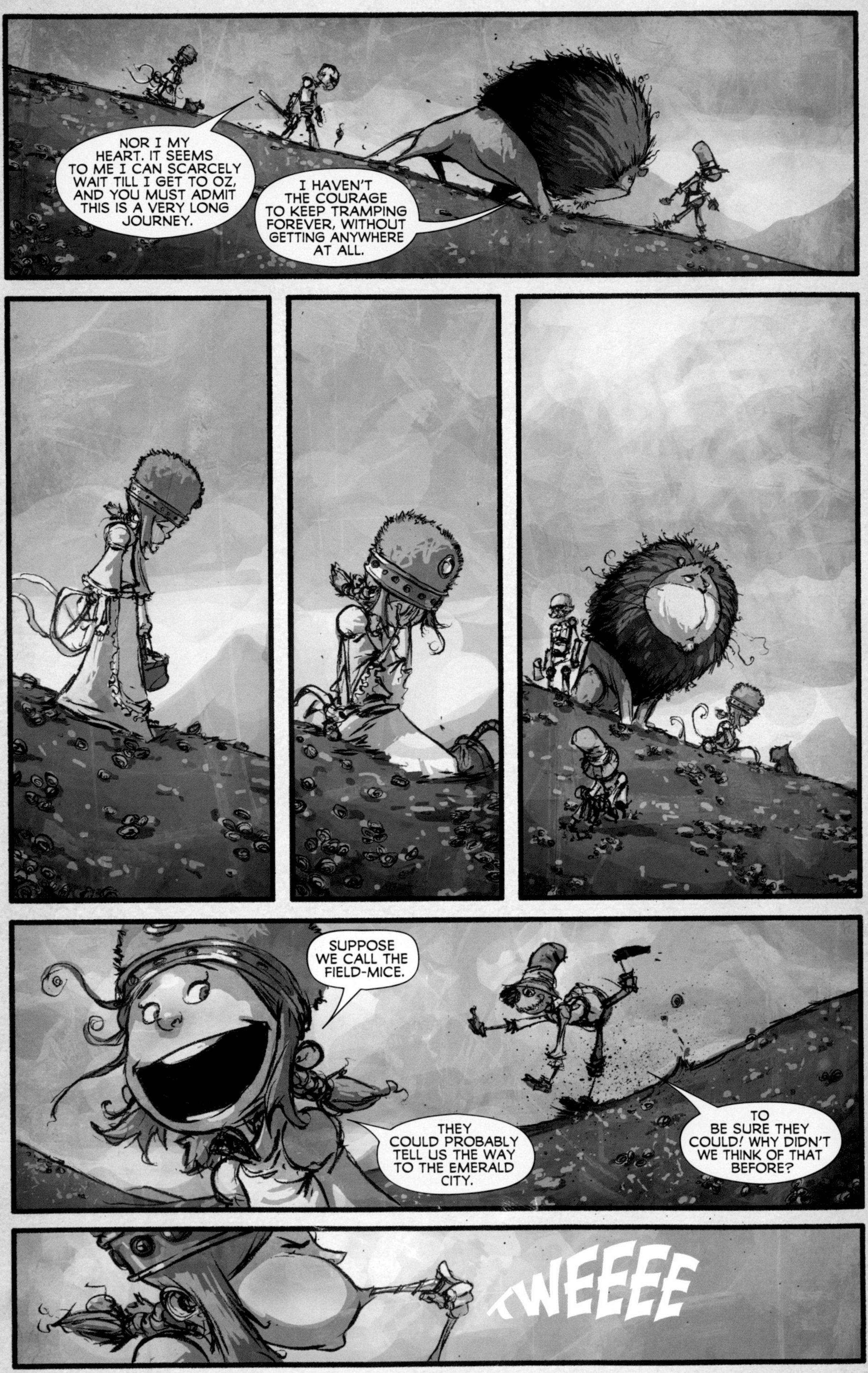
NOR I MY HEART. IT SEEMS TO ME I CAN SCARCELY WAIT TILL I GET TO OZ, AND YOU MUST ADMIT THIS IS A VERY LONG JOURNEY.
I HAVEN'T THE COURAGE TO KEEP TRAMPING FOREVER, WITHOUT GETTING ANYWHERE AT ALL.
SUPPOSE WE CALL THE FIELD-MICE.
THEY COULD PROBABLY TELL US THE WAY TO THE EMERALD CITY.
TO BE SURE THEY COULD! WHY DIDN'T WE THINK OF THAT BEFORE?
TWEEEE

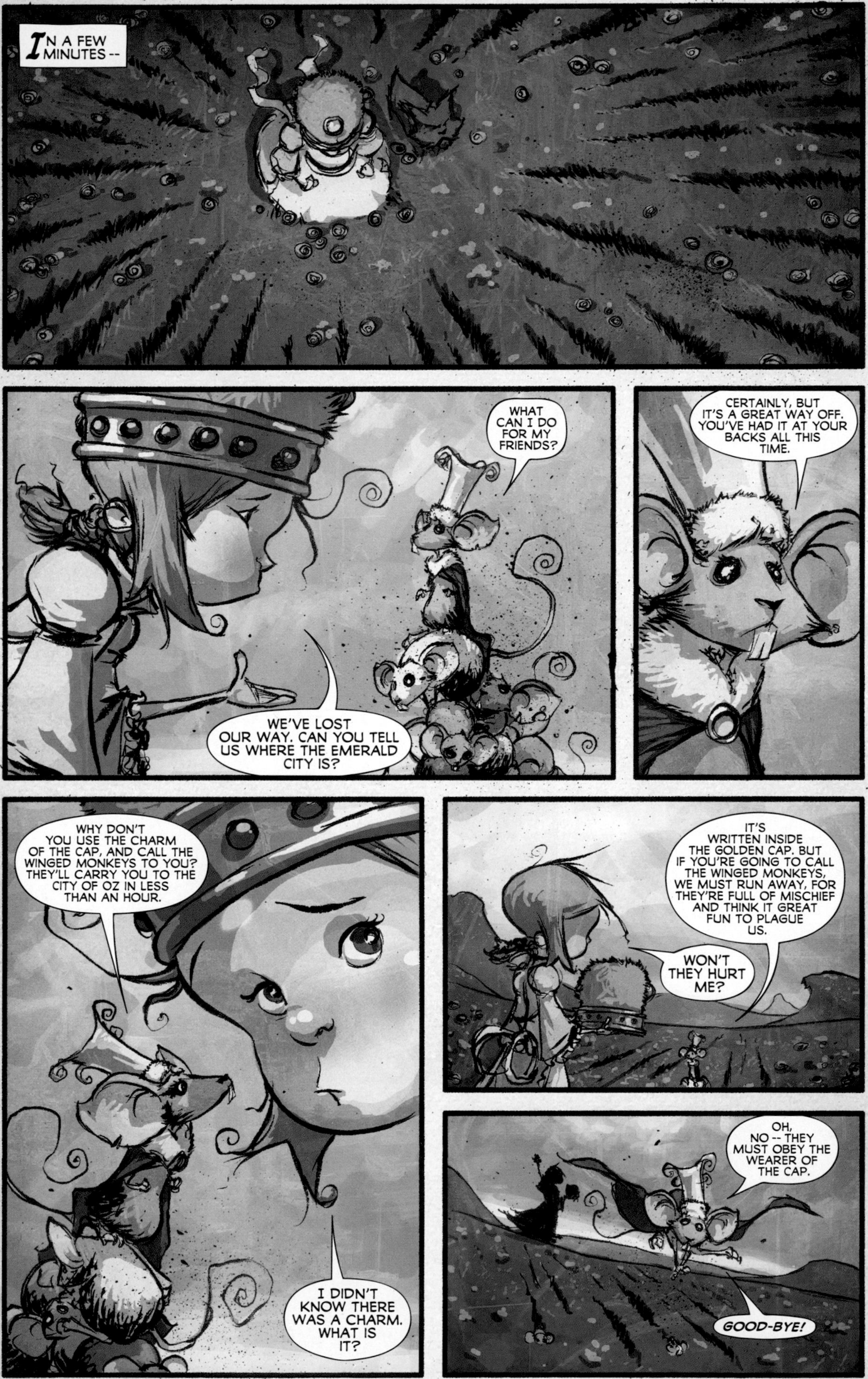
IN A FEW MINUTES --
WHAT CAN I DO FOR MY FRIENDS?
WE'VE LOST OUR WAY. CAN YOU TELL US WHERE THE EMERALD CITY IS?
CERTAINLY, BUT IT'S A GREAT WAY OFF. YOU'VE HAD IT AT YOUR BACKS ALL THIS TIME.
WHY DON'T YOU USE THE CHARM OF THE CAP, AND CALL THE WINGED MONKEYS TO YOU? THEY'LL CARRY YOU TO THE CITY OF OZ IN LESS THAN AN HOUR.
I DIDN'T KNOW THERE WAS A CHARM. WHAT IS IT?
IT'S WRITTEN INSIDE THE GOLDEN CAP. BUT IF YOU'RE GOING TO CALL THE WINGED MONKEYS, WE MUST RUN AWAY, FOR THEY'RE FULL OF MISCHIEF AND THINK IT GREAT FUN TO PLAGUE US.
WON'T THEY HURT ME?
OH, NO -- THEY MUST OBEY THE WEARER OF THE CAP.
GOOD-BYE!

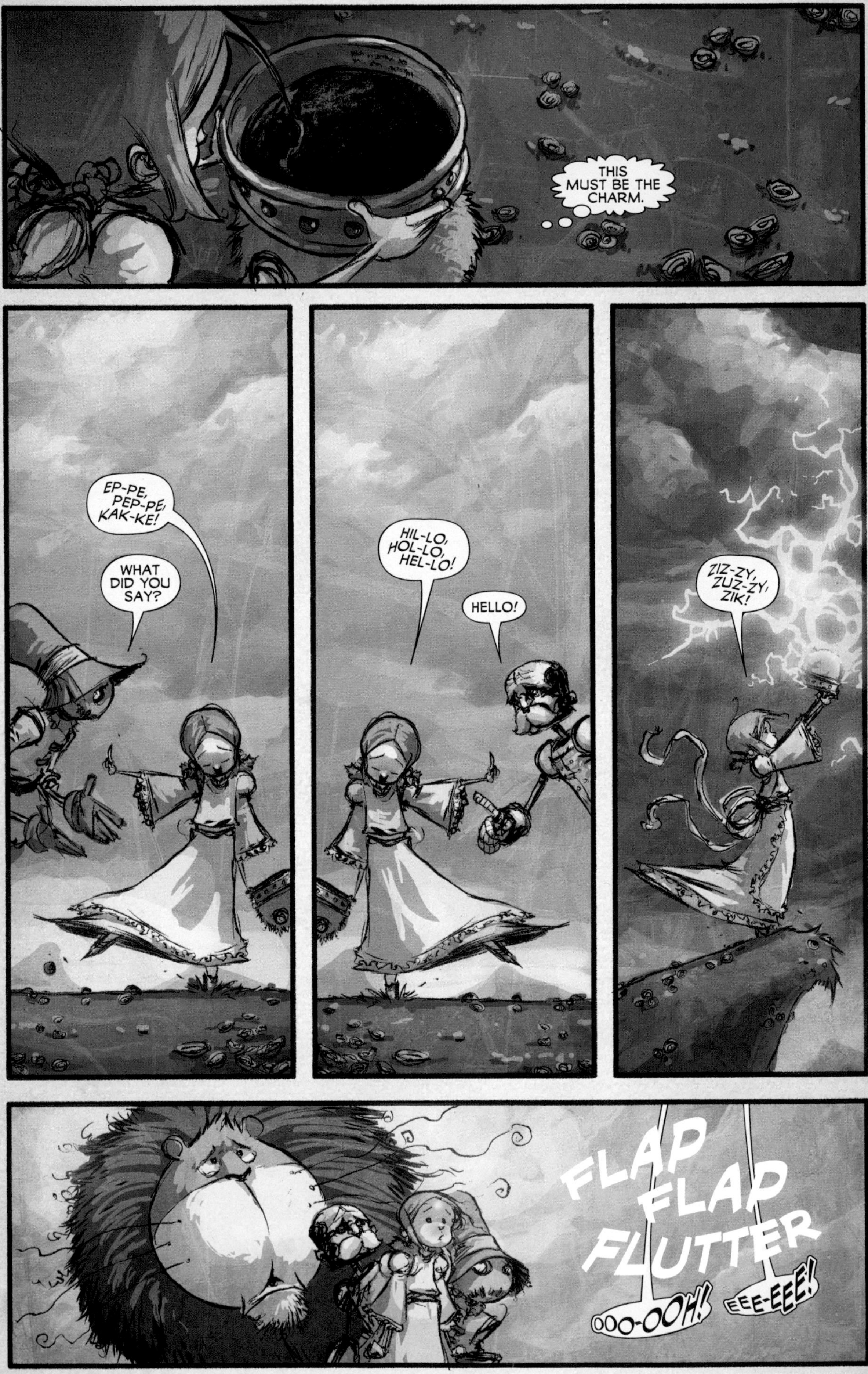
THIS MUST BE THE CHARM.
EP-PE, PEP-PE, KAK-KE!
WHAT DID YOU SAY?
HIL-LO, HOL-LO, HEL-LO!
HELLO!
ZIZ-ZY, ZUZ-ZY, ZIK!
FLAP FLAP FLUTTER
OOO-OOH!
EEE-EEE!

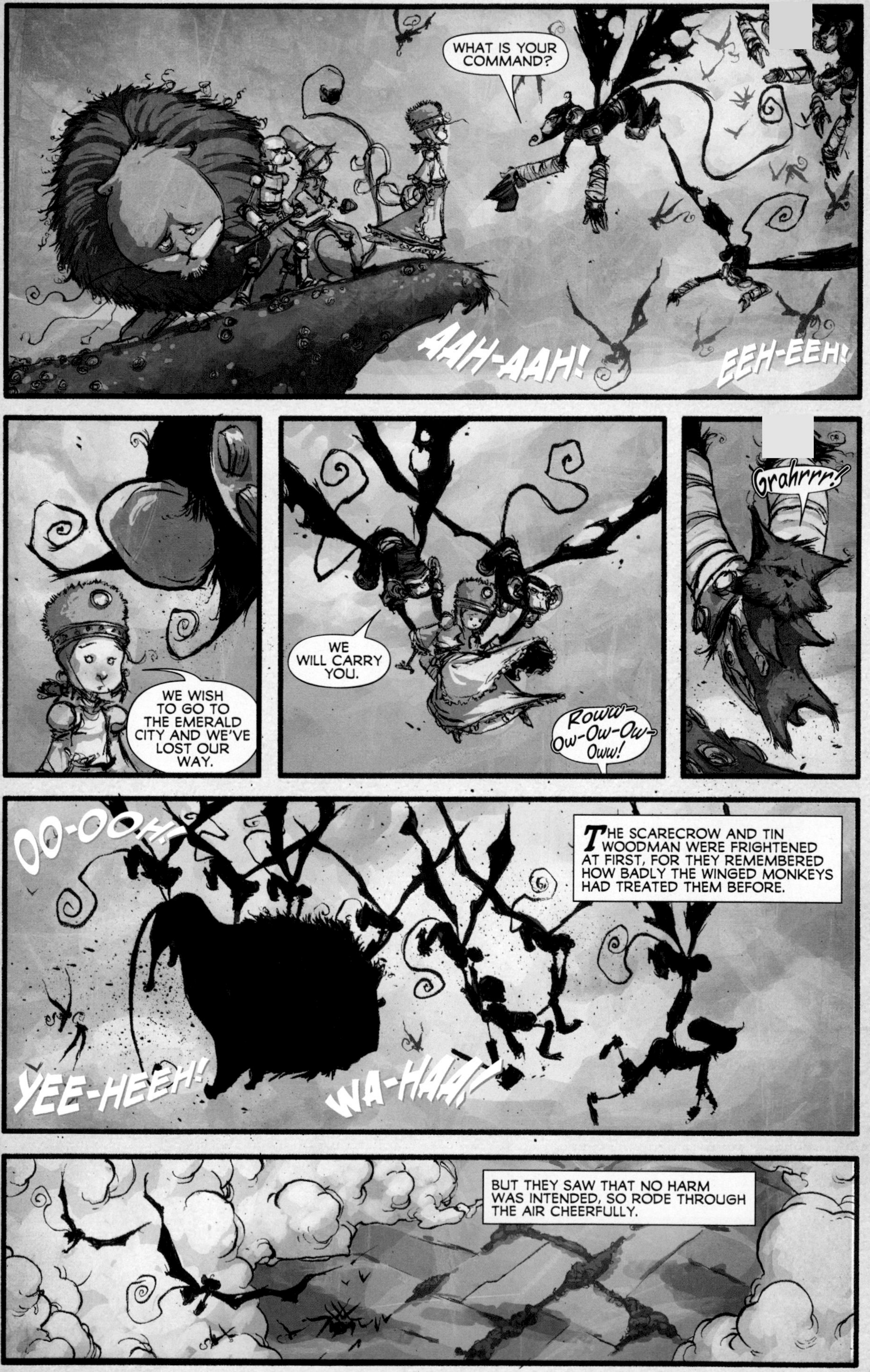
WHAT IS YOUR COMMAND?
AAH-AAH!
EEH-EEH!
WE WISH TO GO TO THE EMERALD CITY AND WE'VE LOST OUR WAY.
WE WILL CARRY YOU.
Roww-Ow-Ow-Ow-Oww!
Grahrrr!
OO-OOH!
THE SCARECROW AND TIN WOODMAN WERE FRIGHTENED AT FIRST, FOR THEY REMEMBERED HOW BADLY THE WINGED MONKEYS HAD TREATED THEM BEFORE.
YEE-HEEH!
WA-HAA!
BUT THEY SAW THAT NO HARM WAS INTENDED, SO RODE THROUGH THE AIR CHEERFULLY.

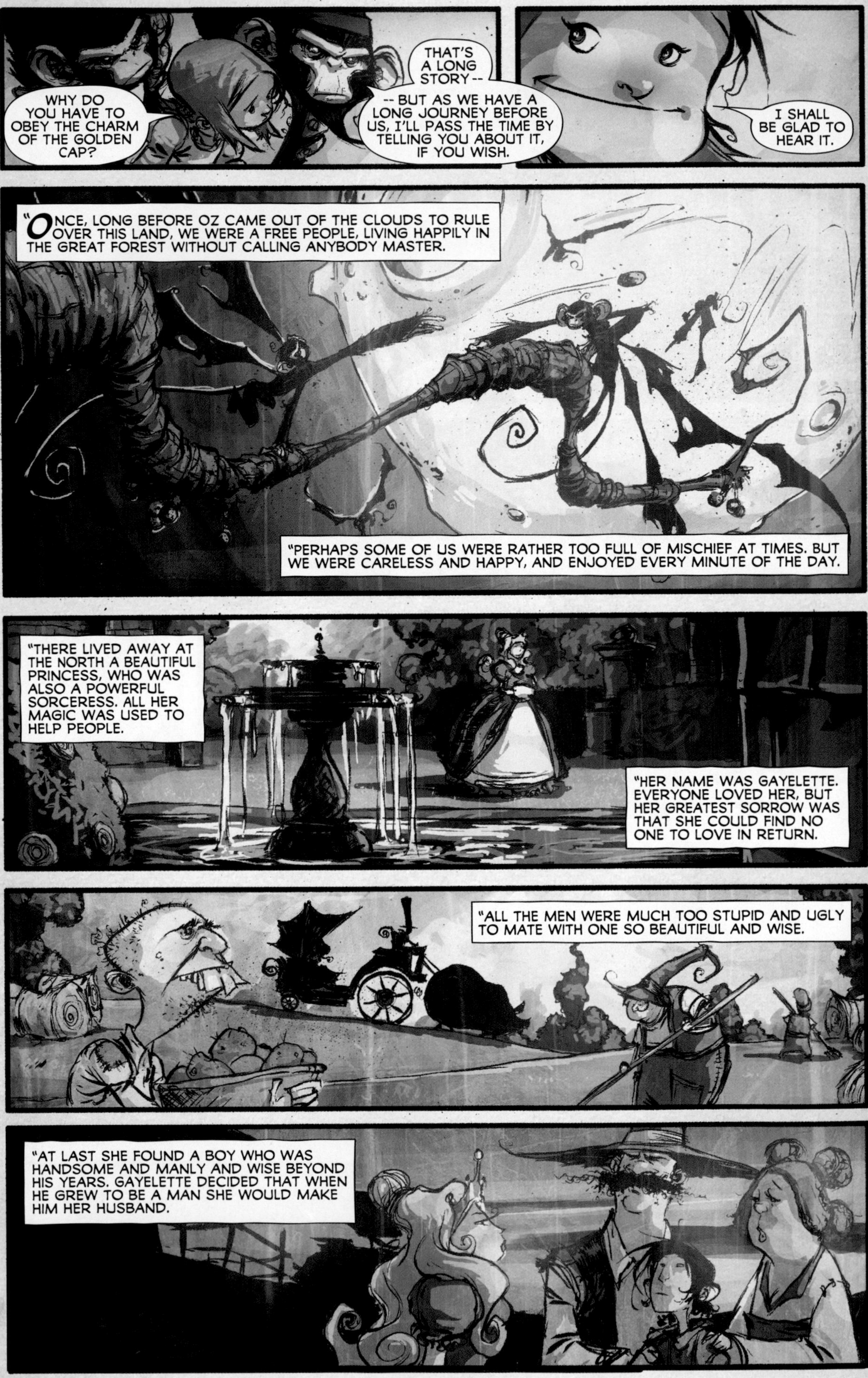
WHY DO YOU HAVE TO OBEY THE CHARM OF THE GOLDEN CAP?
THAT'S A LONG STORY --
-- BUT AS WE HAVE A LONG JOURNEY BEFORE US, I'LL PASS THE TIME BY TELLING YOU ABOUT IT, IF YOU WISH.
I SHALL BE GLAD TO HEAR IT.
"ONCE, LONG BEFORE OZ CAME OUT OF THE CLOUDS TO RULE OVER THIS LAND, WE WERE A FREE PEOPLE, LIVING HAPPILY IN THE GREAT FOREST WITHOUT CALLING ANYBODY MASTER.
"PERHAPS SOME OF US WERE RATHER TOO FULL OF MISCHIEF AT TIMES. BUT WE WERE CARELESS AND HAPPY, AND ENJOYED EVERY MINUTE OF THE DAY.
"THERE LIVED AWAY AT THE NORTH A BEAUTIFUL PRINCESS, WHO WAS ALSO A POWERFUL SORCERESS. ALL HER MAGIC WAS USED TO HELP PEOPLE.
"HER NAME WAS GAYELETTE. EVERYONE LOVED HER, BUT HER GREATEST SORROW WAS THAT SHE COULD FIND NO ONE TO LOVE IN RETURN.
"ALL THE MEN WERE MUCH TOO STUPID AND UGLY TO MATE WITH ONE SO BEAUTIFUL AND WISE.
"AT LAST SHE FOUND A BOY WHO WAS HANDSOME AND MANLY AND WISE BEYOND HIS YEARS. GAYELETTE DECIDED THAT WHEN HE GREW TO BE A MAN SHE WOULD MAKE HIM HER HUSBAND.

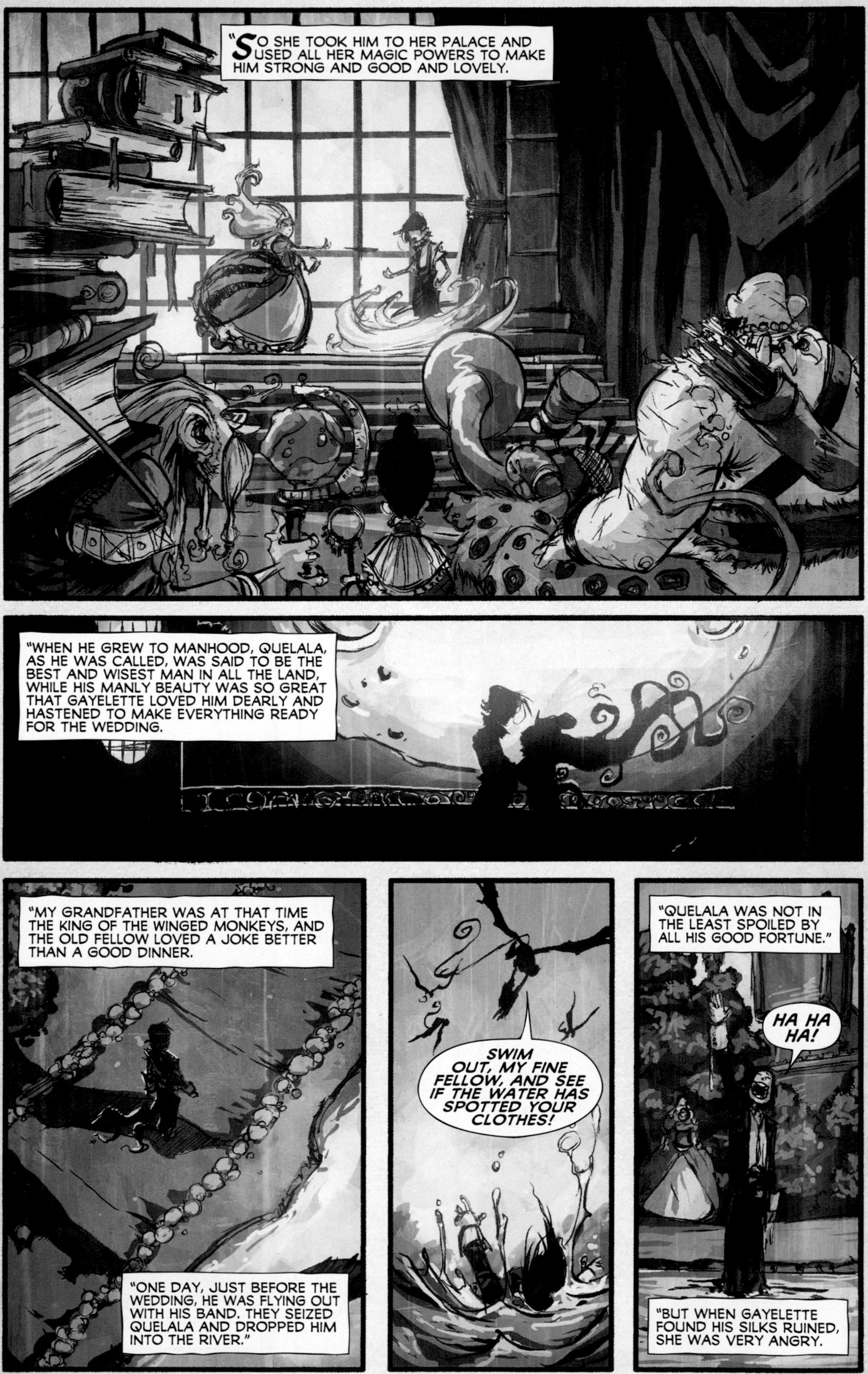
"SO SHE TOOK HIM TO HER PALACE AND USED ALL HER MAGIC POWERS TO MAKE HIM STRONG AND GOOD AND LOVELY.
"WHEN HE GREW TO MANHOOD, QUELALA, AS HE WAS CALLED, WAS SAID TO BE THE BEST AND WISEST MAN IN ALL THE LAND, WHILE HIS MANLY BEAUTY WAS SO GREAT THAT GAYELETTE LOVED HIM DEARLY AND HASTENED TO MAKE EVERYTHING READY FOR THE WEDDING.
"MY GRANDFATHER WAS AT THAT TIME THE KING OF THE WINGED MONKEYS, AND THE OLD FELLOW LOVED A JOKE BETTER THAN A GOOD DINNER.
"ONE DAY, JUST BEFORE THE WEDDING, HE WAS FLYING OUT WITH HIS BAND. THEY SEIZED QUELALA AND DROPPED HIM INTO THE RIVER."
SWIM OUT, MY FINE FELLOW, AND SEE IF THE WATER HAS SPOTTED YOUR CLOTHES!
"QUELALA WAS NOT IN THE LEAST SPOILED BY ALL HIS GOOD FORTUNE."
HA HA HA!
"BUT WHEN GAYELETTE FOUND HIS SILKS RUINED, SHE WAS VERY ANGRY.

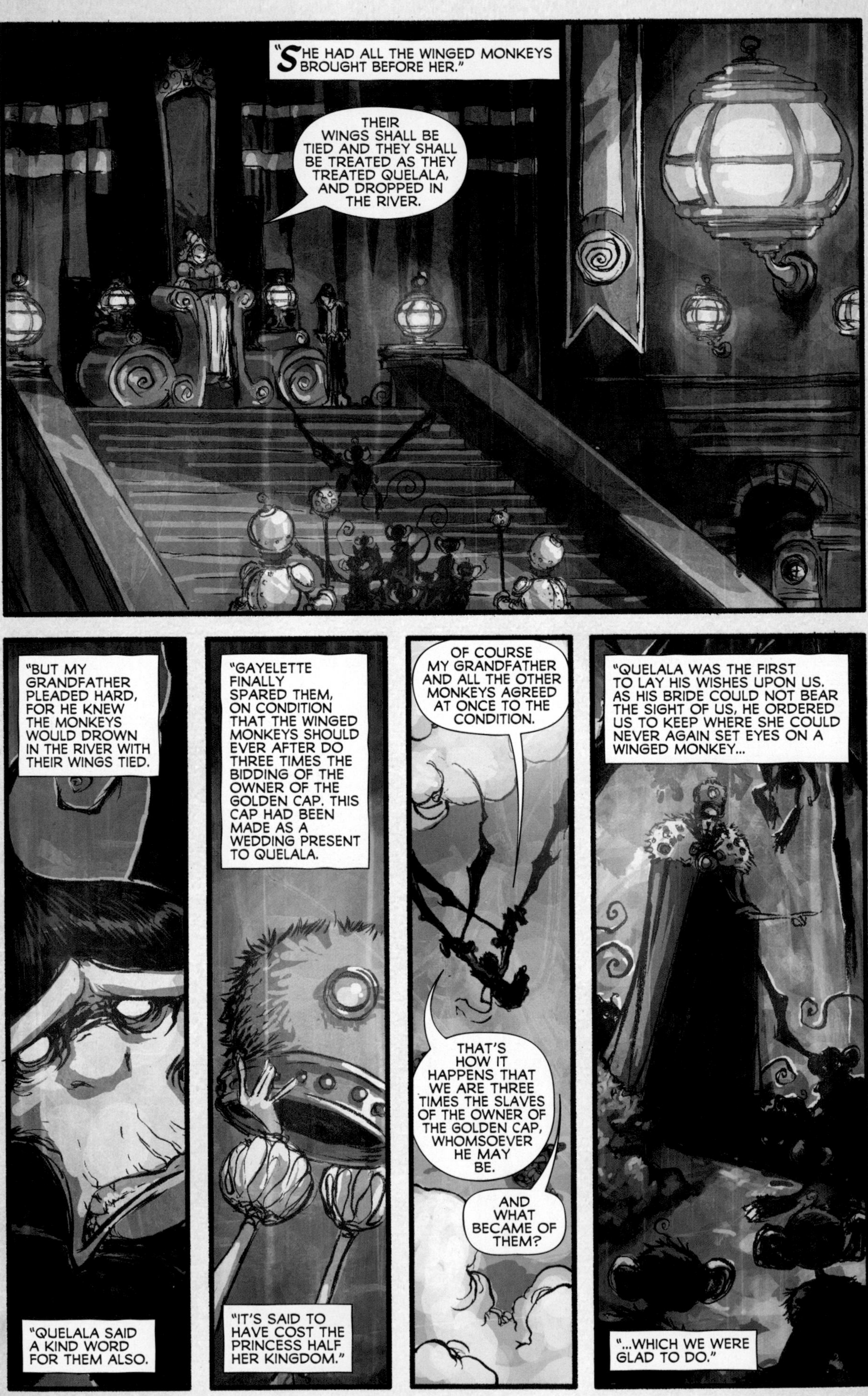
"SHE HAD ALL THE WINGED MONKEYS BROUGHT BEFORE HER."
THEIR WINGS SHALL BE TIED AND THEY SHALL BE TREATED AS THEY TREATED QUELALA, AND DROPPED IN THE RIVER.
"BUT MY GRANDFATHER PLEADED HARD, FOR HE KNEW THE MONKEYS WOULD DROWN IN THE RIVER WITH THEIR WINGS TIED.
"QUELALA SAID A KIND WORD FOR THEM ALSO.
"GAYELETTE FINALLY SPARED THEM, ON CONDITION THAT THE WINGED MONKEYS SHOULD EVER AFTER DO THREE TIMES THE BIDDING OF THE OWNER OF THE GOLDEN CAP. THIS CAP HAD BEEN MADE AS A WEDDING PRESENT TO QUELALA.
"IT'S SAID TO HAVE COST THE PRINCESS HALF HER KINGDOM."
OF COURSE MY GRANDFATHER AND ALL THE OTHER MONKEYS AGREED AT ONCE TO THE CONDITION.
THAT'S HOW IT HAPPENS THAT WE ARE THREE TIMES THE SLAVES OF THE OWNER OF THE GOLDEN CAP, WHOMSOEVER HE MAY BE.
AND WHAT BECAME OF THEM?
"QUELALA WAS THE FIRST TO LAY HIS WISHES UPON US. AS HIS BRIDE COULD NOT BEAR THE SIGHT OF US, HE ORDERED US TO KEEP WHERE SHE COULD NEVER AGAIN SET EYES ON A WINGED MONKEY...
"...WHICH WE WERE GLAD TO DO."

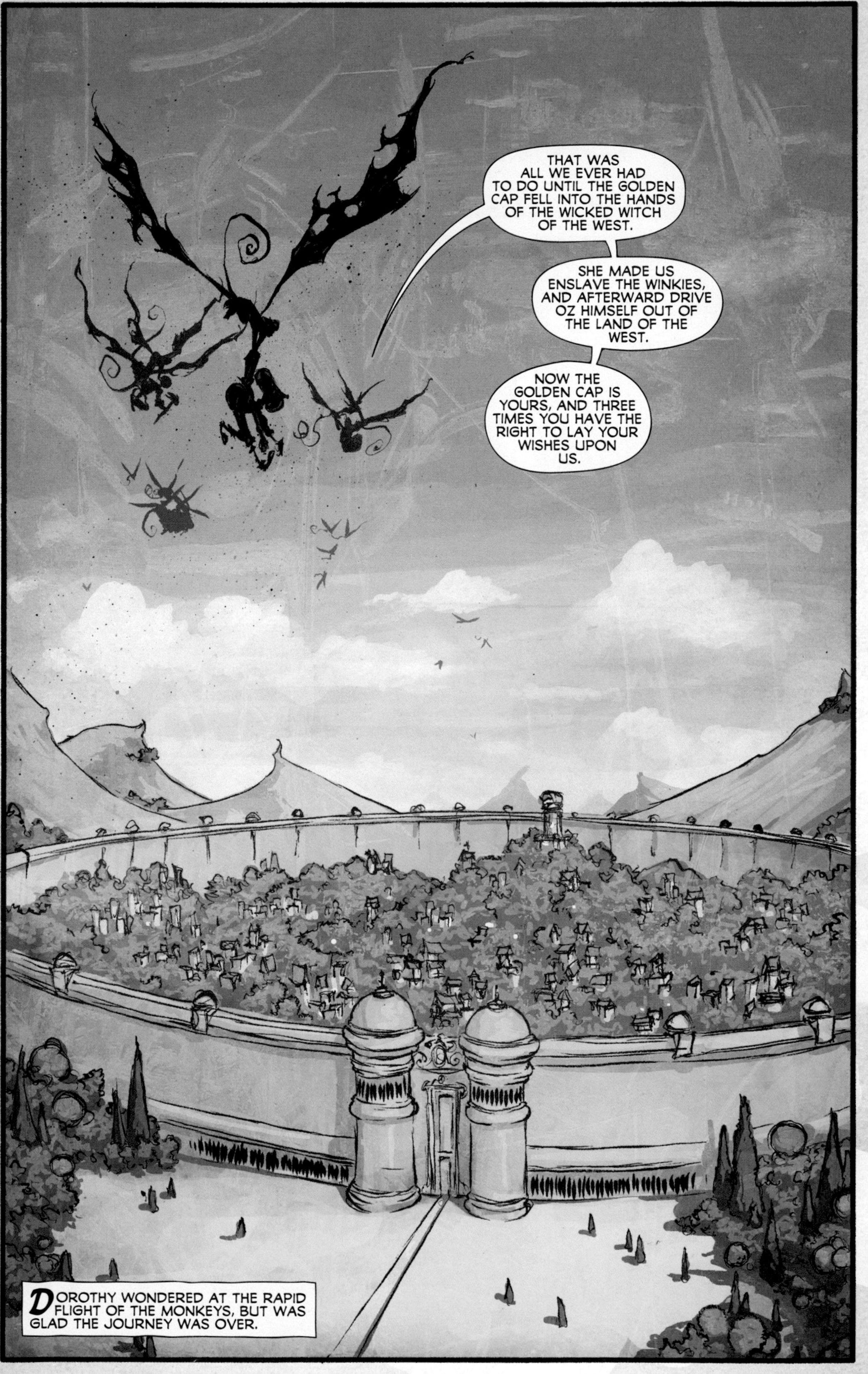
THAT WAS ALL WE EVER HAD TO DO UNTIL THE GOLDEN CAP FELL INTO THE HANDS OF THE WICKED WITCH OF THE WEST.
SHE MADE US ENSLAVE THE WINKIES, AND AFTERWARD DRIVE OZ HIMSELF OUT OF THE LAND OF THE WEST.
NOW THE GOLDEN CAP IS YOURS, AND THREE TIMES YOU HAVE THE RIGHT TO LAY YOUR WISHES UPON US.
DOROTHY WONDERED AT THE RAPID FLIGHT OF THE MONKEYS, BUT WAS GLAD THE JOURNEY WAS OVER.

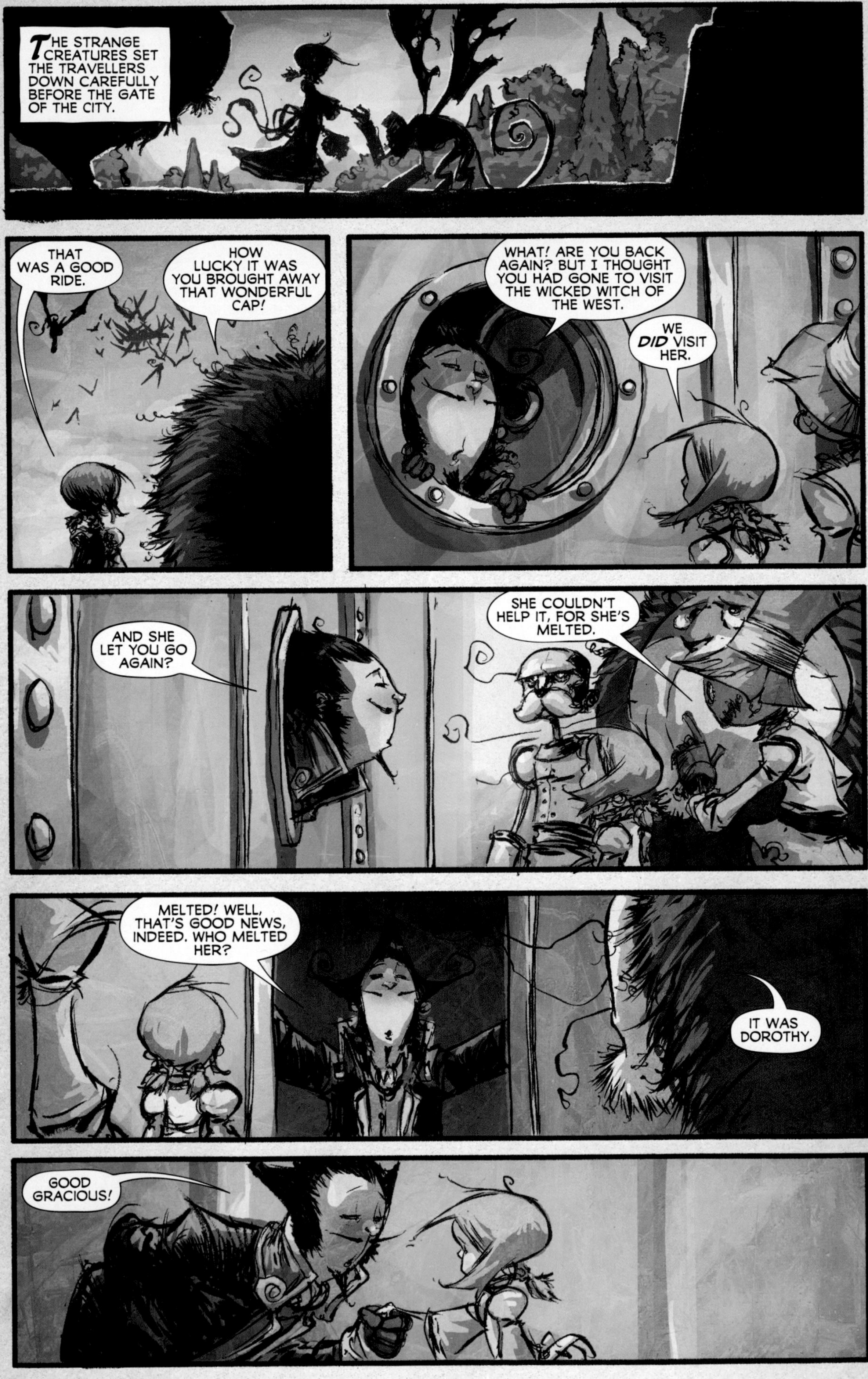
THE STRANGE CREATURES SET THE TRAVELLERS DOWN CAREFULLY BEFORE THE GATE OF THE CITY.
THAT WAS A GOOD RIDE.
HOW LUCKY IT WAS YOU BROUGHT AWAY THAT WONDERFUL CAP!
WHAT! ARE YOU BACK AGAIN? BUT I THOUGHT YOU HAD GONE TO VISIT THE WICKED WITCH OF THE WEST.
WE DID VISIT HER.
AND SHE LET YOU GO AGAIN?
SHE COULDN'T HELP IT, FOR SHE'S MELTED.
MELTED! WELL, THAT'S GOOD NEWS, INDEED. WHO MELTED HER?
IT WAS DOROTHY.
GOOD GRACIOUS!

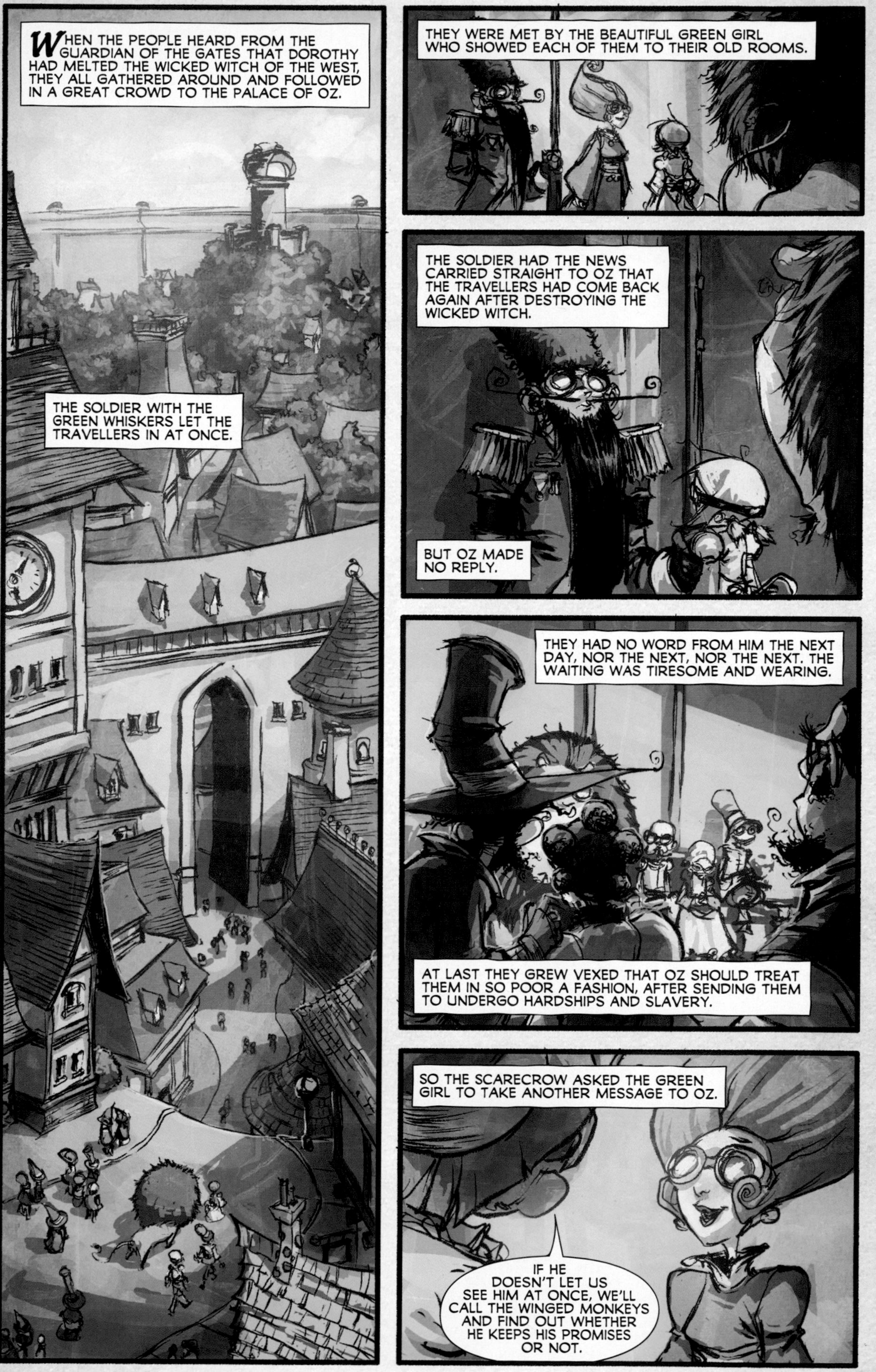

WHEN THE PEOPLE HEARD FROM THE GUARDIAN OF THE GATES THAT DOROTHY HAD MELTED THE WICKED WITCH OF THE WEST, THEY ALL GATHERED AROUND AND FOLLOWED IN A GREAT CROWD TO THE PALACE OF OZ.
THE SOLDIER WITH THE GREEN WHISKERS LET THE TRAVELLERS IN AT ONCE.
THEY WERE MET BY THE BEAUTIFUL GREEN GIRL WHO SHOWED EACH OF THEM TO THEIR OLD ROOMS.
THE SOLDIER HAD THE NEWS CARRIED STRAIGHT TO OZ THAT THE TRAVELLERS HAD COME BACK AGAIN AFTER DESTROYING THE WICKED WITCH.
BUT OZ MADE NO REPLY.
THEY HAD NO WORD FROM HIM THE NEXT DAY, NOR THE NEXT, NOR THE NEXT. THE WAITING WAS TIRESOME AND WEARING.
AT LAST THEY GREW VEXED THAT OZ SHOULD TREAT THEM IN SO POOR A FASHION, AFTER SENDING THEM TO UNDERGO HARDSHIPS AND SLAVERY.
SO THE SCARECROW ASKED THE GREEN GIRL TO TAKE ANOTHER MESSAGE TO OZ.
IF HE DOESN'T LET US SEE HIM AT ONCE, WE'LL CALL THE WINGED MONKEYS AND FIND OUT WHETHER HE KEEPS HIS PROMISES OR NOT.

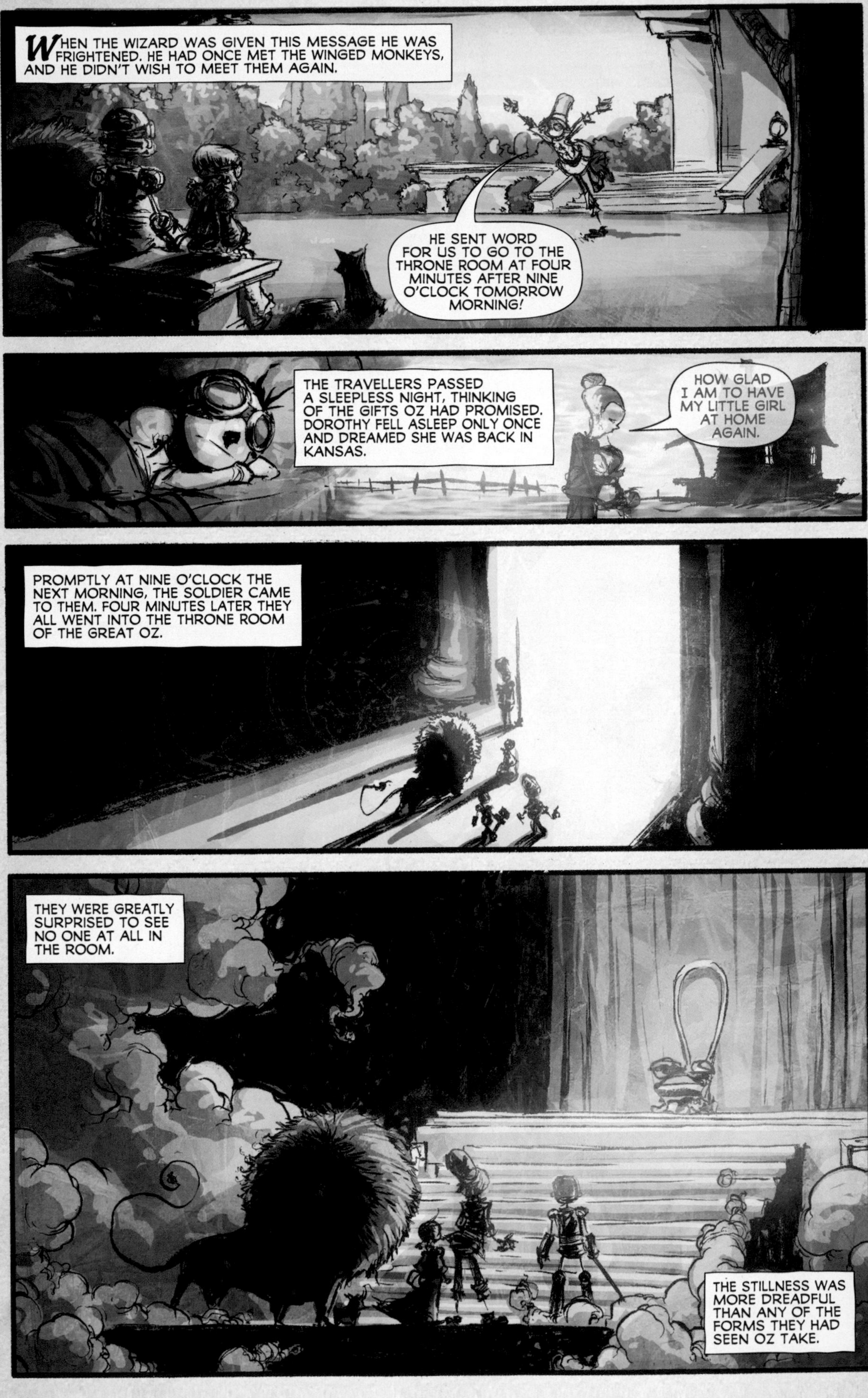
WHEN THE WIZARD WAS GIVEN THIS MESSAGE HE WAS FRIGHTENED. HE HAD ONCE MET THE WINGED MONKEYS, AND HE DIDN'T WISH TO MEET THEM AGAIN.
HE SENT WORD FOR US TO GO TO THE THRONE ROOM AT FOUR MINUTES AFTER NINE O'CLOCK TOMORROW MORNING!
THE TRAVELLERS PASSED A SLEEPLESS NIGHT, THINKING OF THE GIFTS OZ HAD PROMISED. DOROTHY FELL ASLEEP ONLY ONCE AND DREAMED SHE WAS BACK IN KANSAS.
HOW GLAD I AM TO HAVE MY LITTLE GIRL AT HOME AGAIN.
PROMPTLY AT NINE O'CLOCK THE NEXT MORNING, THE SOLDIER CAME TO THEM. FOUR MINUTES LATER THEY ALL WENT INTO THE THRONE ROOM OF THE GREAT OZ.
THEY WERE GREATLY SURPRISED TO SEE NO ONE AT ALL IN THE ROOM.
THE STILLNESS WAS MORE DREADFUL THAN ANY OF THE FORMS THEY HAD SEEN OZ TAKE.

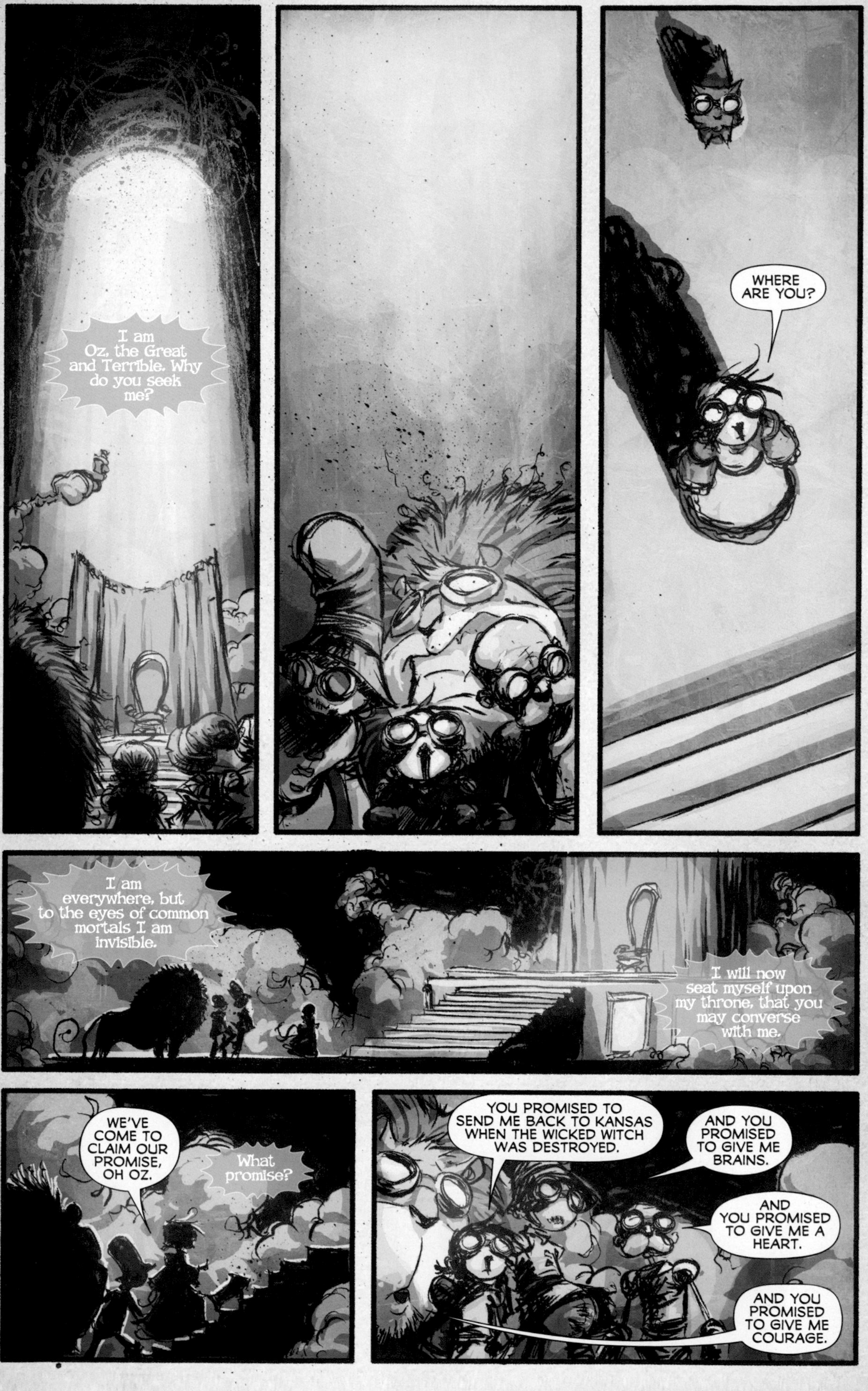
I am Oz, the Great and Terrible. Why do you seek me?
WHERE ARE YOU?
I am everywhere, but to the eyes of common mortals I am invisible.
I will now seat myself upon my throne, that you may converse with me.
WE'VE COME TO CLAIM OUR PROMISE, OH OZ.
What promise?
YOU PROMISED TO SEND ME BACK TO KANSAS WHEN THE WICKED WITCH WAS DESTROYED.
AND YOU PROMISED TO GIVE ME BRAINS.
AND YOU PROMISED TO GIVE ME A HEART.
AND YOU PROMISED TO GIVE ME COURAGE.

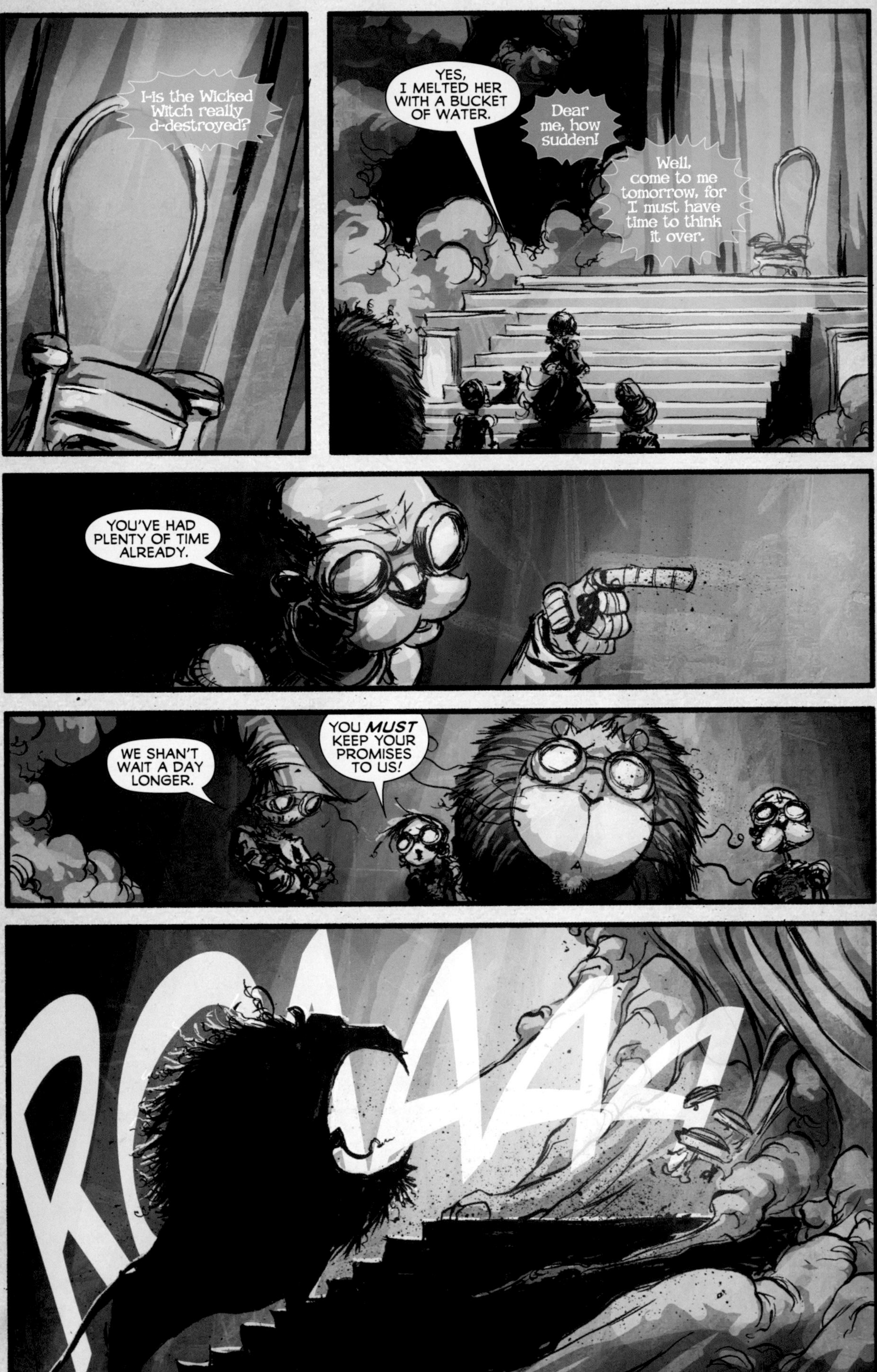

I-is the Wicked Witch really d-destroyed?
YES, I MELTED HER WITH A BUCKET OF WATER.
Dear me, how sudden!
Well, come to me tomorrow, for I must have time to think it over.
YOU'VE HAD PLENTY OF TIME ALREADY.
WE SHAN'T WAIT A DAY LONGER.
YOU MUST KEEP YOUR PROMISES TO US!
ROAAAA

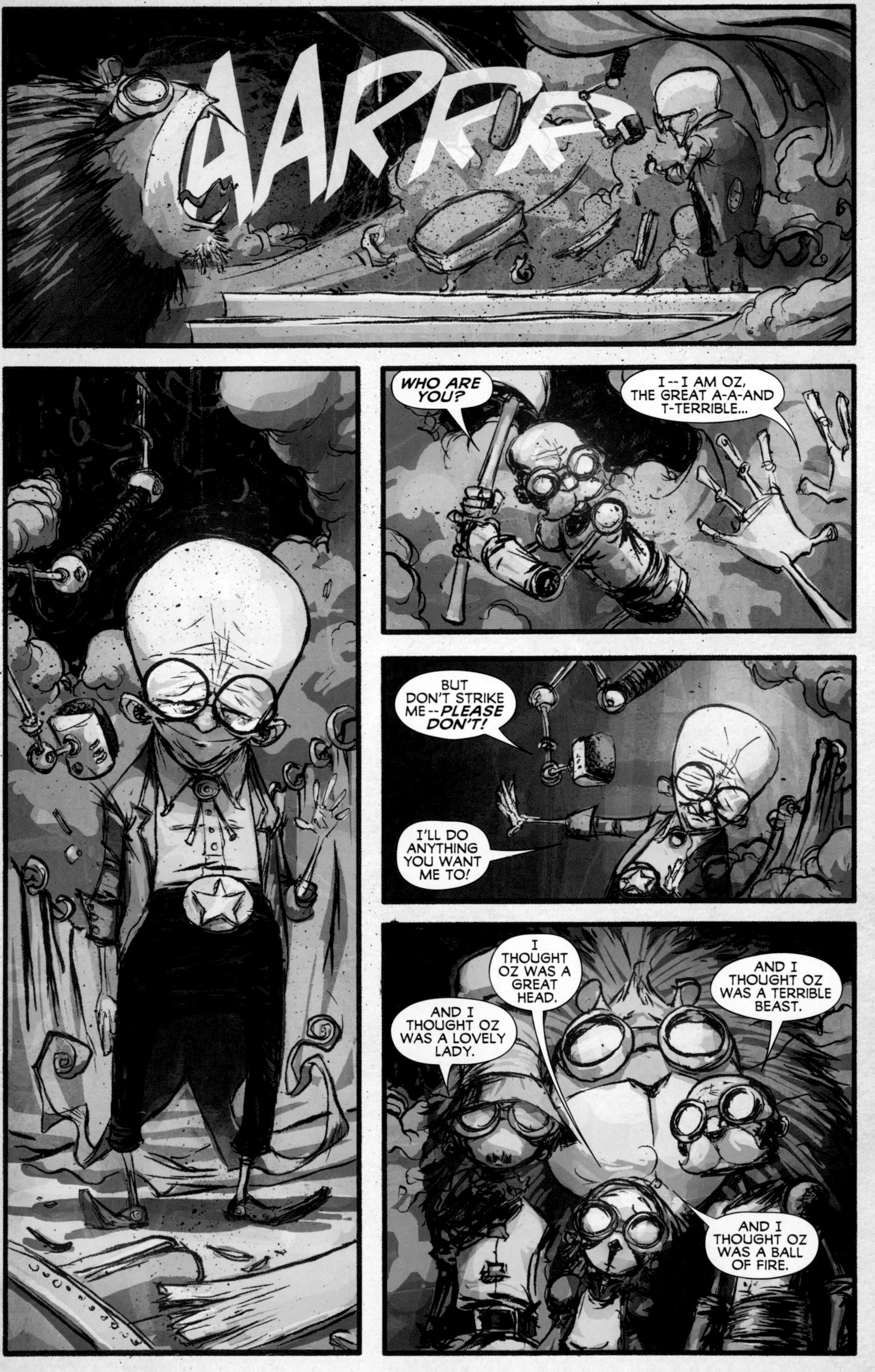
AARRR
WHO ARE YOU?
I -- I AM OZ, THE GREAT A-A-AND T-TERRIBLE...
BUT DON'T STRIKE ME -- PLEASE DON'T!
I'LL DO ANYTHING YOU WANT ME TO!
AND I THOUGHT OZ WAS A LOVELY LADY.
I THOUGHT OZ WAS A GREAT HEAD.
AND I THOUGHT OZ WAS A TERRIBLE BEAST.
AND I THOUGHT OZ WAS A BALL OF FIRE.

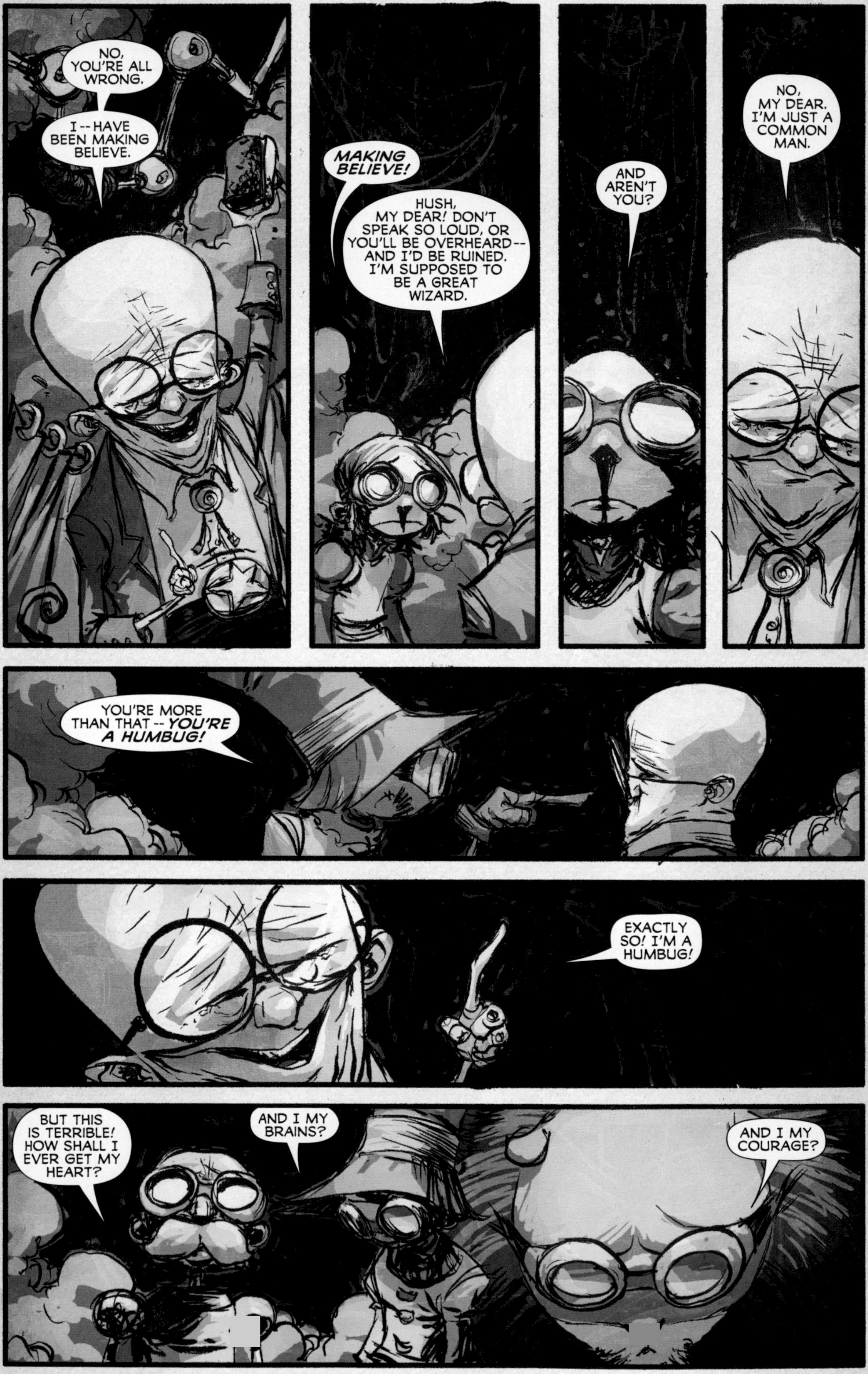
NO, YOU'RE ALL WRONG.
I -- HAVE BEEN MAKING BELIEVE.
MAKING BELIEVE!
HUSH, MY DEAR! DON'T SPEAK SO LOUD, OR YOU'LL BE OVERHEARD -- AND I'D BE RUINED. I'M SUPPOSED TO BE A GREAT WIZARD.
AND AREN'T YOU?
NO, MY DEAR. I'M JUST A COMMON MAN.
YOU'RE MORE THAN THAT -- *YOU'RE A HUMBUG!*
EXACTLY SO! I'M A HUMBUG!
BUT THIS IS TERRIBLE! HOW SHALL I EVER GET MY HEART?
AND I MY BRAINS?
AND I MY COURAGE?

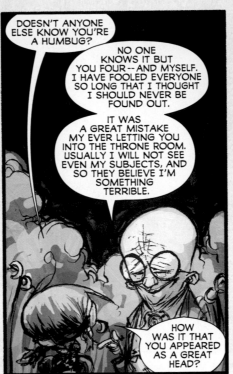

MY DEAR FRIENDS, I PRAY YOU NOT TO SPEAK OF THESE LITTLE THINGS.

THINK OF ME, AND THE TERRIBLE TROUBLE I'M IN AT BEING FOUND OUT.

DOESN'T ANYONE ELSE KNOW YOU'RE A HUMBUG?

NO ONE KNOWS IT BUT YOU FOUR -- AND MYSELF. I HAVE FOOLED EVERYONE SO LONG THAT I THOUGHT I SHOULD NEVER BE FOUND OUT.

IT WAS A GREAT MISTAKE MY EVER LETTING YOU INTO THE THRONE ROOM. USUALLY I WILL NOT SEE EVEN MY SUBJECTS, AND SO THEY BELIEVE I'M SOMETHING TERRIBLE.

HOW WAS IT THAT YOU APPEARED AS A GREAT HEAD?

THAT WAS ONE OF MY TRICKS. STEP THIS WAY, PLEASE.

OH, I'M A VENTRILOQUIST, AND I CAN THROW THE SOUND OF MY VOICE WHEREVER I WISH, SO THAT YOU THOUGHT IT WAS COMING OUT OF THE HEAD.

THIS I HUNG FROM THE CEILING BY A WIRE. I STOOD BEHIND THE SCREEN AND PULLED A THREAD, TO MAKE THE EYES MOVE AND THE MOUTH OPEN.

BUT HOW ABOUT THE VOICE?

HERE ARE THE OTHER THINGS I USED TO DECEIVE YOU.

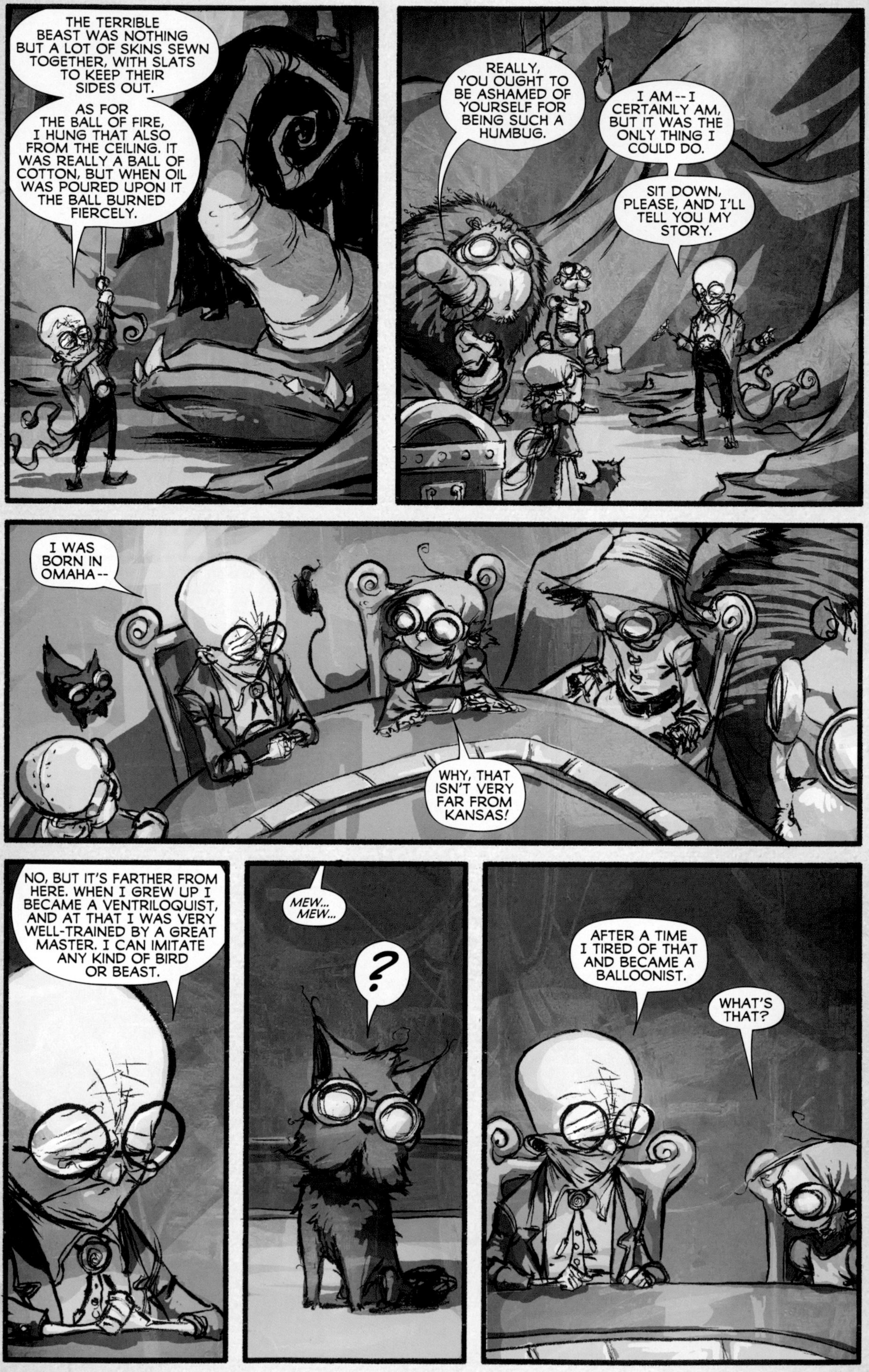
THE TERRIBLE BEAST WAS NOTHING BUT A LOT OF SKINS SEWN TOGETHER, WITH SLATS TO KEEP THEIR SIDES OUT.
AS FOR THE BALL OF FIRE, I HUNG THAT ALSO FROM THE CEILING. IT WAS REALLY A BALL OF COTTON, BUT WHEN OIL WAS POURED UPON IT THE BALL BURNED FIERCELY.
REALLY, YOU OUGHT TO BE ASHAMED OF YOURSELF FOR BEING SUCH A HUMBUG.
I AM--I CERTAINLY AM, BUT IT WAS THE ONLY THING I COULD DO.
SIT DOWN, PLEASE, AND I'LL TELL YOU MY STORY.
I WAS BORN IN OMAHA--
WHY, THAT ISN'T VERY FAR FROM KANSAS!
NO, BUT IT'S FARTHER FROM HERE. WHEN I GREW UP I BECAME A VENTRILOQUIST, AND AT THAT I WAS VERY WELL-TRAINED BY A GREAT MASTER. I CAN IMITATE ANY KIND OF BIRD OR BEAST.
MEW... MEW...
?
AFTER A TIME I TIRED OF THAT AND BECAME A BALLOONIST.
WHAT'S THAT?

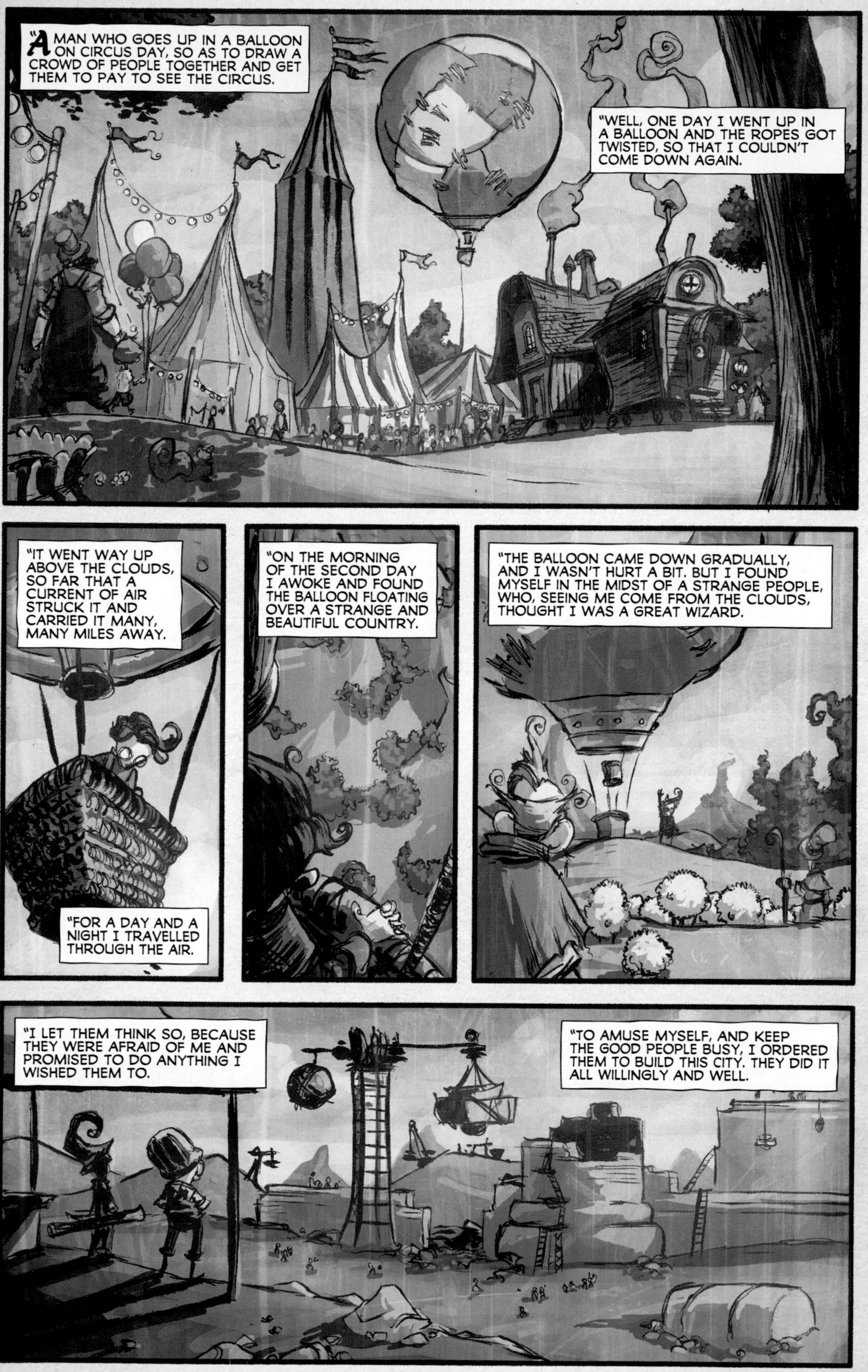
"A MAN WHO GOES UP IN A BALLOON ON CIRCUS DAY, SO AS TO DRAW A CROWD OF PEOPLE TOGETHER AND GET THEM TO PAY TO SEE THE CIRCUS.
"WELL, ONE DAY I WENT UP IN A BALLOON AND THE ROPES GOT TWISTED, SO THAT I COULDN'T COME DOWN AGAIN.
"IT WENT WAY UP ABOVE THE CLOUDS, SO FAR THAT A CURRENT OF AIR STRUCK IT AND CARRIED IT MANY, MANY MILES AWAY.
"FOR A DAY AND A NIGHT I TRAVELLED THROUGH THE AIR.
"ON THE MORNING OF THE SECOND DAY I AWOKE AND FOUND THE BALLOON FLOATING OVER A STRANGE AND BEAUTIFUL COUNTRY.
"THE BALLOON CAME DOWN GRADUALLY, AND I WASN'T HURT A BIT. BUT I FOUND MYSELF IN THE MIDST OF A STRANGE PEOPLE, WHO, SEEING ME COME FROM THE CLOUDS, THOUGHT I WAS A GREAT WIZARD.
"I LET THEM THINK SO, BECAUSE THEY WERE AFRAID OF ME AND PROMISED TO DO ANYTHING I WISHED THEM TO.
"TO AMUSE MYSELF, AND KEEP THE GOOD PEOPLE BUSY, I ORDERED THEM TO BUILD THIS CITY. THEY DID IT ALL WILLINGLY AND WELL.

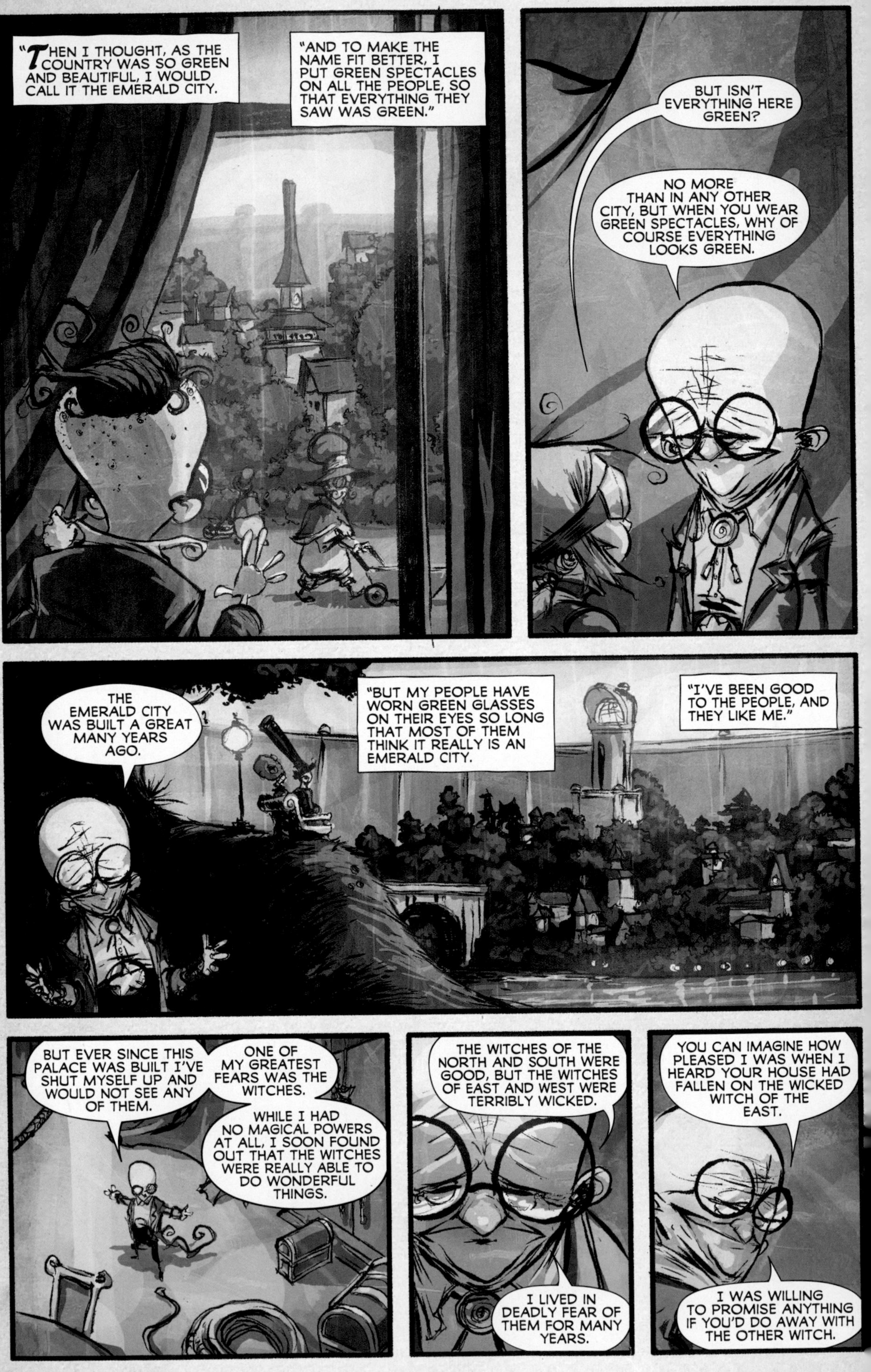
"THEN I THOUGHT, AS THE COUNTRY WAS SO GREEN AND BEAUTIFUL, I WOULD CALL IT THE EMERALD CITY.
"AND TO MAKE THE NAME FIT BETTER, I PUT GREEN SPECTACLES ON ALL THE PEOPLE, SO THAT EVERYTHING THEY SAW WAS GREEN."
BUT ISN'T EVERYTHING HERE GREEN?
NO MORE THAN IN ANY OTHER CITY, BUT WHEN YOU WEAR GREEN SPECTACLES, WHY OF COURSE EVERYTHING LOOKS GREEN.
THE EMERALD CITY WAS BUILT A GREAT MANY YEARS AGO.
"BUT MY PEOPLE HAVE WORN GREEN GLASSES ON THEIR EYES SO LONG THAT MOST OF THEM THINK IT REALLY IS AN EMERALD CITY.
"I'VE BEEN GOOD TO THE PEOPLE, AND THEY LIKE ME."
BUT EVER SINCE THIS PALACE WAS BUILT I'VE SHUT MYSELF UP AND WOULD NOT SEE ANY OF THEM.
ONE OF MY GREATEST FEARS WAS THE WITCHES.
WHILE I HAD NO MAGICAL POWERS AT ALL, I SOON FOUND OUT THAT THE WITCHES WERE REALLY ABLE TO DO WONDERFUL THINGS.
THE WITCHES OF THE NORTH AND SOUTH WERE GOOD, BUT THE WITCHES OF EAST AND WEST WERE TERRIBLY WICKED.
I LIVED IN DEADLY FEAR OF THEM FOR MANY YEARS.
YOU CAN IMAGINE HOW PLEASED I WAS WHEN I HEARD YOUR HOUSE HAD FALLEN ON THE WICKED WITCH OF THE EAST.
I WAS WILLING TO PROMISE ANYTHING IF YOU'D DO AWAY WITH THE OTHER WITCH.

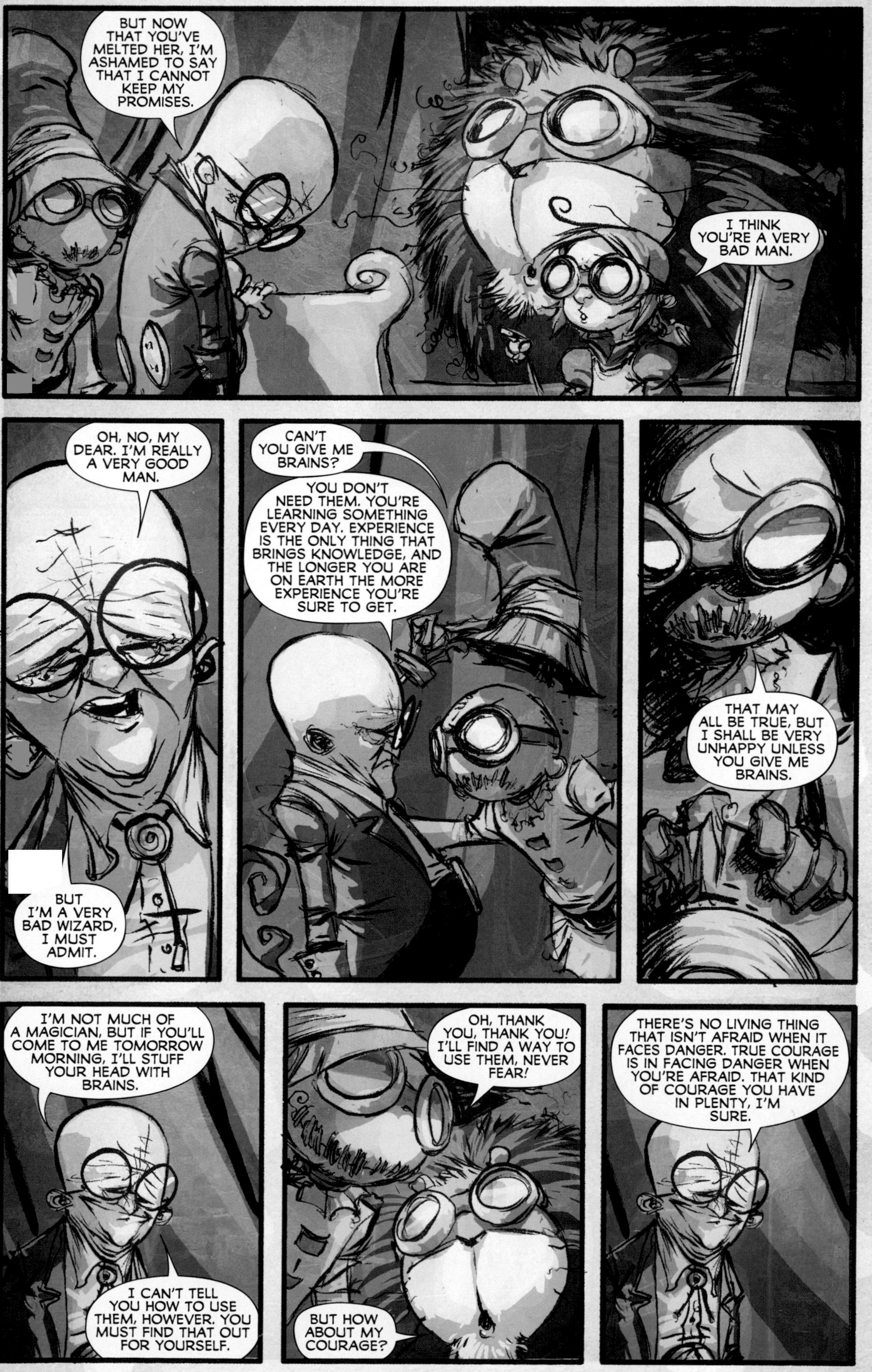
BUT NOW THAT YOU'VE MELTED HER, I'M ASHAMED TO SAY THAT I CANNOT KEEP MY PROMISES.
I THINK YOU'RE A VERY BAD MAN.
OH, NO, MY DEAR. I'M REALLY A VERY GOOD MAN.
BUT I'M A VERY BAD WIZARD, I MUST ADMIT.
CAN'T YOU GIVE ME BRAINS?
YOU DON'T NEED THEM. YOU'RE LEARNING SOMETHING EVERY DAY. EXPERIENCE IS THE ONLY THING THAT BRINGS KNOWLEDGE, AND THE LONGER YOU ARE ON EARTH THE MORE EXPERIENCE YOU'RE SURE TO GET.
THAT MAY ALL BE TRUE, BUT I SHALL BE VERY UNHAPPY UNLESS YOU GIVE ME BRAINS.
I'M NOT MUCH OF A MAGICIAN, BUT IF YOU'LL COME TO ME TOMORROW MORNING, I'LL STUFF YOUR HEAD WITH BRAINS.
I CAN'T TELL YOU HOW TO USE THEM, HOWEVER. YOU MUST FIND THAT OUT FOR YOURSELF.
OH, THANK YOU, THANK YOU! I'LL FIND A WAY TO USE THEM, NEVER FEAR!
BUT HOW ABOUT MY COURAGE?
THERE'S NO LIVING THING THAT ISN'T AFRAID WHEN IT FACES DANGER. TRUE COURAGE IS IN FACING DANGER WHEN YOU'RE AFRAID. THAT KIND OF COURAGE YOU HAVE IN PLENTY, I'M SURE.

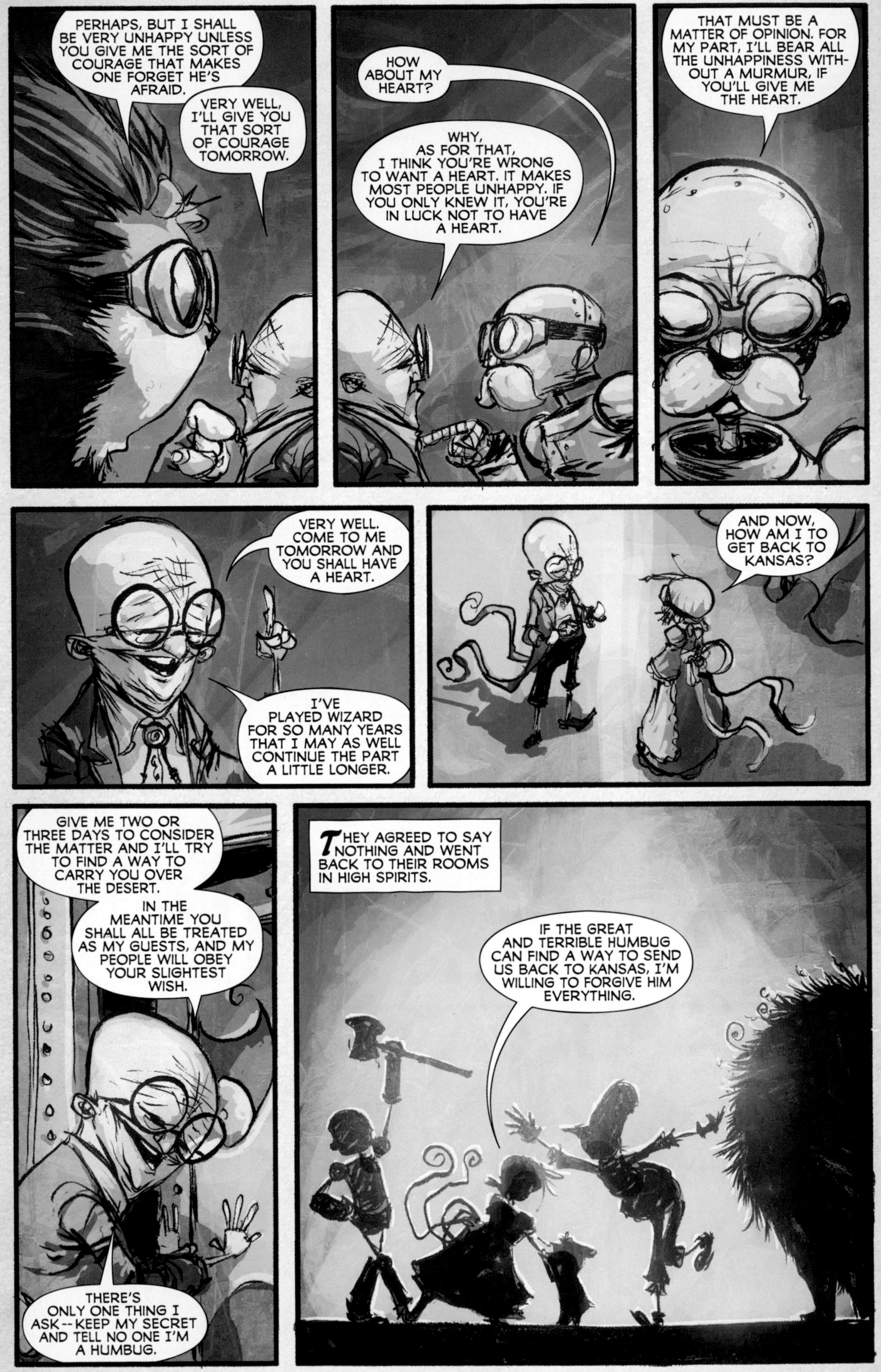
PERHAPS, BUT I SHALL BE VERY UNHAPPY UNLESS YOU GIVE ME THE SORT OF COURAGE THAT MAKES ONE FORGET HE'S AFRAID.
VERY WELL, I'LL GIVE YOU THAT SORT OF COURAGE TOMORROW.
HOW ABOUT MY HEART?
WHY, AS FOR THAT, I THINK YOU'RE WRONG TO WANT A HEART. IT MAKES MOST PEOPLE UNHAPPY. IF YOU ONLY KNEW IT, YOU'RE IN LUCK NOT TO HAVE A HEART.
THAT MUST BE A MATTER OF OPINION. FOR MY PART, I'LL BEAR ALL THE UNHAPPINESS WITH-OUT A MURMUR, IF YOU'LL GIVE ME THE HEART.
VERY WELL. COME TO ME TOMORROW AND YOU SHALL HAVE A HEART.
I'VE PLAYED WIZARD FOR SO MANY YEARS THAT I MAY AS WELL CONTINUE THE PART A LITTLE LONGER.
AND NOW, HOW AM I TO GET BACK TO KANSAS?
GIVE ME TWO OR THREE DAYS TO CONSIDER THE MATTER AND I'LL TRY TO FIND A WAY TO CARRY YOU OVER THE DESERT.
IN THE MEANTIME YOU SHALL ALL BE TREATED AS MY GUESTS, AND MY PEOPLE WILL OBEY YOUR SLIGHTEST WISH.
THERE'S ONLY ONE THING I ASK--KEEP MY SECRET AND TELL NO ONE I'M A HUMBUG.
THEY AGREED TO SAY NOTHING AND WENT BACK TO THEIR ROOMS IN HIGH SPIRITS.
IF THE GREAT AND TERRIBLE HUMBUG CAN FIND A WAY TO SEND US BACK TO KANSAS, I'M WILLING TO FORGIVE HIM EVERYTHING.